THE ADVENTURES OF TOM SAWYER

by MARK TWAIN

#4 The Spelling Bee

Adapted by Catherine Nichols

Illustrated by Amy Bates

Sterling Publishing Co., Inc.
New York

Library of Congress Cataloging-in-Publication Data Available

10 9 8 7 6 5 4 3 2

Published by Sterling Publishing Co., Inc.
387 Park Avenue South, New York, NY 10016
Copyright © 2007 by Sterling Publishing Co., Inc.
Illustrations © 2007 by Amy Bates
Distributed in Canada by Sterling Publishing
c/o Canadian Manda Group, 165 Dufferin Street
Toronto, Ontario, Canada M6K 3H6
Distributed in the United Kingdom by GMC Distribution Services
Castle Place, 166 High Street, Lewes, East Sussex, England BN7 1XU
Distributed in Australia by Capricorn Link (Australia) Pty. Ltd.
P.O. Box 704, Windsor, NSW 2756, Australia

Printed in China

Sterling ISBN-13: 978-1-4027-4269-9
        ISBN-10: 1-4027-4269-X

For information about custom editions, special sales, premium
and corporate purchases, please contact Sterling Special Sales
Department at 800-805-5489 or specialsales@sterlingpub.com.

Contents

The New Girl

It was Monday morning.
Time for school!
Tom Sawyer was running
as fast as he could.
He didn't want to be late.

Tom ran past
a big tree.
A sign was on it.
It said that the circus
was coming to town.

Tom stopped running.
How he wished he could
go to the circus!
Too bad he had spent
all his allowance!

The bell was ringing.

Tom made it to class

just in time.

There was a seat next to

Becky Thatcher, the new girl.

Tom hurried to sit in it.

"Hello, Tom," Becky said.

She smiled at him.

Tom felt his face get hot.

Everyone said Becky was

the prettiest girl in school.

"Hello, Becky," Tom said.
Then he buried his face
in his lesson book.

Mr. Masters was
their teacher.
"I have a surprise,
class," he said.
"We are having
a spelling bee.
The winner will get
a ticket to the circus."

The class turned
to look at Edward.
Edward was the
smartest boy in school.
He always won
the spelling bees.

Tom looked at Becky.
Now she was smiling
at Edward—not Tom.
Right then and there,
Tom decided *he* would
win the spelling bee . . .
even if it meant studying
his spelling words!

Tom and Becky

The spelling bee was
later that afternoon.
Tom studied during lunch.
He studied during recess, too.
He studied the spelling words
until he knew them backward
and forward. Tom had never
studied so much in his life!

At last it was time.
The students stood
next to their desks.
Whoever spelled
a word wrong
had to sit down.

The last one standing
would be the winner.
Tom was so nervous,
he couldn't keep still.

Tom got his first word right.

He got his next word right.

He got the one after that right.

Soon, Tom, Edward, and Becky
were the only ones left standing.

Then it was Edward's turn.

To everyone's surprise,

he did not spell his word right!

Now it was between

Tom and Becky.

Who would be

the winner?

The Winner

Mr. Masters put down
the spelling list.
"We have used up the words
on this list," he said.
"We must use a new list."
He took out another paper.
Oh, no! thought Tom.
I did not study *that* list!

"It is your turn, Tom,"
Mr. Masters said.
"Spell *circus*."
Tom gulped.
He wanted to *go*
to the circus . . .
but he could not *spell* it!

"Tom?" said Mr. Masters.

Tom gulped again.

He looked out the window.

He saw a clown walking by.

The clown was carrying a sign.

It said, "Come see the circus."

There it is! thought Tom.

That's the word I need to spell!

Tom looked around
to make sure no one
had seen the sign.
Then he said,
"Circus. C–I–R–C–U–S."
"That is correct,"
said Mr. Masters.

Then it was Becky's turn.
Her word was *cheater.*
"Cheater," Becky said.
"C-H-E-E-T-E-R."

"I'm sorry, Becky,"
said Mr. Masters.
"That is not correct."
Becky sat down.
Tom was the only one
still standing.
He had won the contest!

Doing the Right Thing

Mr. Masters handed
Tom the ticket.
Tom was going
to the circus!
All his friends
shook his hand.
They told him
what a good job
he had done.

Becky came up to him.
She looked very sad.
"I so wanted to go
to the circus," she said,
"but you deserve the prize.
You are a good speller."

"You were good, too,"
Tom told Becky.
She shook her head.
"I couldn't spell *cheater*,"
she said. "I bet *you* can.
You are so smart!"

Tom gulped.

He did not feel smart.

He felt awful.

He might not know

how to spell *cheater*,

but he knew what one was.

"*I* am a cheater, Becky!"
Tom burst out.
"I saw the word *circus*
on a sign outside.
That's how I won!"

Tom apologized
and gave Becky the ticket.
Tom was very sad.
No circus for him!
Plus, Becky would probably
never smile at him again!

Tom could not look at Becky
when he gave her the ticket.
"Thank you," he heard her say.
"Now I have something for *you*."

"For *me?*" Tom asked.

"Yes!" said Becky.

Then she gave Tom

not only a big smile . . .

but a big hug, too!

"What was that for?"

Tom asked in surprise.

"That, Tom," she said,

"was for doing the right thing."